韩素和格妮杜

Hansel and Gretel

Retold by Manju Gregory
Illustrated by Jago

Mandarin translation by Sylvia Denham

MANTRA LINGUA

在很久以前，有一个很穷的樵夫，他与他的妻子和两名孩子住在一起。
男孩子的名字叫韩素，他的妹妹的名字叫格妮杜。
当时各地都正在闹饥荒。有一天晚上，那位父亲对他的妻子叹道：
「我们没有足够的面包粮食。」
「听我说，」他的妻子说，「我们将孩子带到树林，然后把他们留在那里，
他们会照顾自己的。」
「但他们可能会被猛兽撕开吞噬啊！」他哭道。
「难道你想我们都一齐死吗？」她说。那樵夫的妻子不停的说，
直至他同意为止。

Once upon a time, long ago, there lived a poor woodcutter with his wife and two children.
The boy's name was Hansel and his sister's, Gretel. At this time a great and terrible famine
had spread throughout the land. One evening the father turned to his wife and sighed,
"There is scarcely enough bread to feed us."
"Listen to me," said his wife. "We will take the children into the wood and leave them there.
They can take care of themselves."

"But they could be torn apart by wild beasts!" he cried.
"Do you want us all to die?" she said. And the man's wife
went on and on and on, until he agreed.

两个小孩一直醒着，坐立不安，又饥饿，又脆弱，
他们听到每一个字，格妮杜更流下凄苦的眼泪。
「不用担心，」韩素说，「我知道怎样救我们。」
他踮着脚走到花园去，在月光下，小径上光亮雪白的卵石被照耀得像银币一样，
韩素将袋口放满卵石，然后回去安慰他的妹妹。

The two children lay awake, restless and weak with hunger.
They had heard every word, and Gretel wept bitter tears.
"Don't worry," said Hansel, "I think I know how we can save ourselves."
He tiptoed out into the garden. Under the light of the moon, bright white pebbles shone like silver coins on the pathway. Hansel filled his pockets with pebbles and returned to comfort his sister.

第二天早上，太阳还未升起，妈妈便把韩素和格妮杜摇醒，「起来，我们要到树林去，给你们每人一块面包，但不要一次过把整块面包吃了。」

他们一起出发，韩素多次停下回望家园。

「你做什么？」他的爸爸大声叫道。

「我只是向那坐在屋顶上的小白猫挥手说再会。」

「荒谬！」他的妈妈答道，「讲老实话，那是晨早的太阳照耀着烟囱。」

其实韩素沿着树林小径走时，一直悄悄地将卵石丢掉到地上去。

Early next morning, even before sunrise, the mother shook Hansel and Gretel awake.
"Get up, we are going into the wood. Here's a piece of bread for each of you, but don't eat it all at once."
They all set off together. Hansel stopped every now and then and looked back towards his home.
"What are you doing?" shouted his father.
"Only waving goodbye to my little white cat who sits on the roof."
"Rubbish!" replied his mother. "Speak the truth. That is the morning sun shining on the chimney pot."
Secretly Hansel was dropping white pebbles along the pathway.

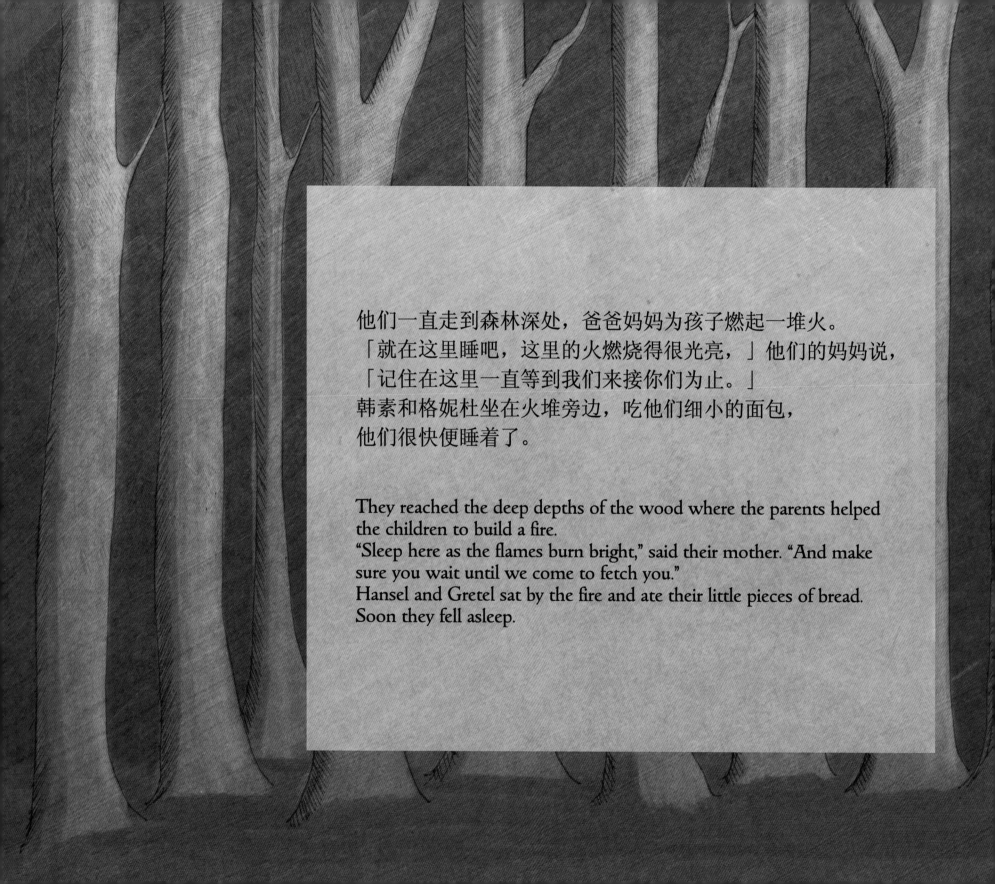

他们一直走到森林深处，爸爸妈妈为孩子燃起一堆火。
「就在这里睡吧，这里的火燃烧得很光亮，」他们的妈妈说，
「记住在这里一直等到我们来接你们为止。」
韩素和格妮杜坐在火堆旁边，吃他们细小的面包，
他们很快便睡着了。

They reached the deep depths of the wood where the parents helped
the children to build a fire.
"Sleep here as the flames burn bright," said their mother. "And make
sure you wait until we come to fetch you."
Hansel and Gretel sat by the fire and ate their little pieces of bread.
Soon they fell asleep.

当他们醒来时，树林已是漆黑一片。

格妮杜哭得很可怜，「我们怎样回家啊？」

「只要等到月满高升时，」韩素说，「我们便会见到闪耀的卵石了。」

格妮杜看着黑暗转为月光，她握着她哥哥的手一起走，

靠着卵石闪耀着的光觅路而行。

When they awoke the woods were pitch black.
Gretel cried miserably, "How will we get home?"
"Just wait until the full moon rises," said Hansel. "Then we will see the shiny pebbles."
Gretel watched the darkness turn to moonlight. She held her brother's hand and together
they walked, finding their way by the light of the glittering pebbles.

将近天亮时，他们便到达樵夫的小屋。
当妈妈打开门时，她大声叫道：
「为什么你们在树林睡了那么久？
我还以为你们不再回家了。」
她很愤怒，不过他们的爸爸却很高兴，
他根本不想把他们留下独自离去。

过了一段时间，家中的粮食依然不足够。
一天晚上，韩素和格妮杜听到他们的母亲说：「孩子一定要走，
我们就把他们带到树林更深之处，这次他们便不能再找到出路了。」
韩素悄悄地走下床，准备再去收集卵石，但这次房门却上了锁。
「不要哭，」他告诉格妮杜说，「我会想办法的，睡觉吧。」

Towards morning they reached the woodcutter's cottage.
As she opened the door their mother yelled, "Why have you slept so long in the woods?
I thought you were never coming home."
She was furious, but their father was happy. He had hated leaving them all alone.

Time passed. Still there was not enough food to feed the family.
One night Hansel and Gretel overheard their mother saying, "The children must go.
We will take them further into the woods. This time they will not find their way out."
Hansel crept from his bed to collect pebbles again but this time the door was locked.
"Don't cry," he told Gretel. "I will think of something. Go to sleep now."

第二天，他们带着更加细块的面包上路，孩子被带领到他们从来未去过的森林深处。

韩素不住停下来，将面包碎丢到地上。

爸爸和妈妈燃起火堆后便叫他们睡觉，「我们现在去砍柴，做完工作后便回来带你们走，」妈妈说。

格妮杜与她的哥哥吃过面包后便一直等，但始终都没有人来。

「当月亮升起时，我们便会看到面包碎，那时就可以寻路回家了，」韩素说。

月亮升起来，但却见不到面包碎，树林的雀鸟和动物都把面包碎吃光了。

The next day, with even smaller pieces of bread for their journey, the children were led to a place deep in the woods where they had never been before. Every now and then Hansel stopped and threw crumbs onto the ground.

Their parents lit a fire and told them to sleep. "We are going to cut wood, and will fetch you when the work is done," said their mother.

Gretel shared her bread with Hansel and they both waited and waited. But no one came.

"When the moon rises we'll see the crumbs of bread and find our way home," said Hansel.

The moon rose but the crumbs were gone.

The birds and animals of the wood had eaten every one.

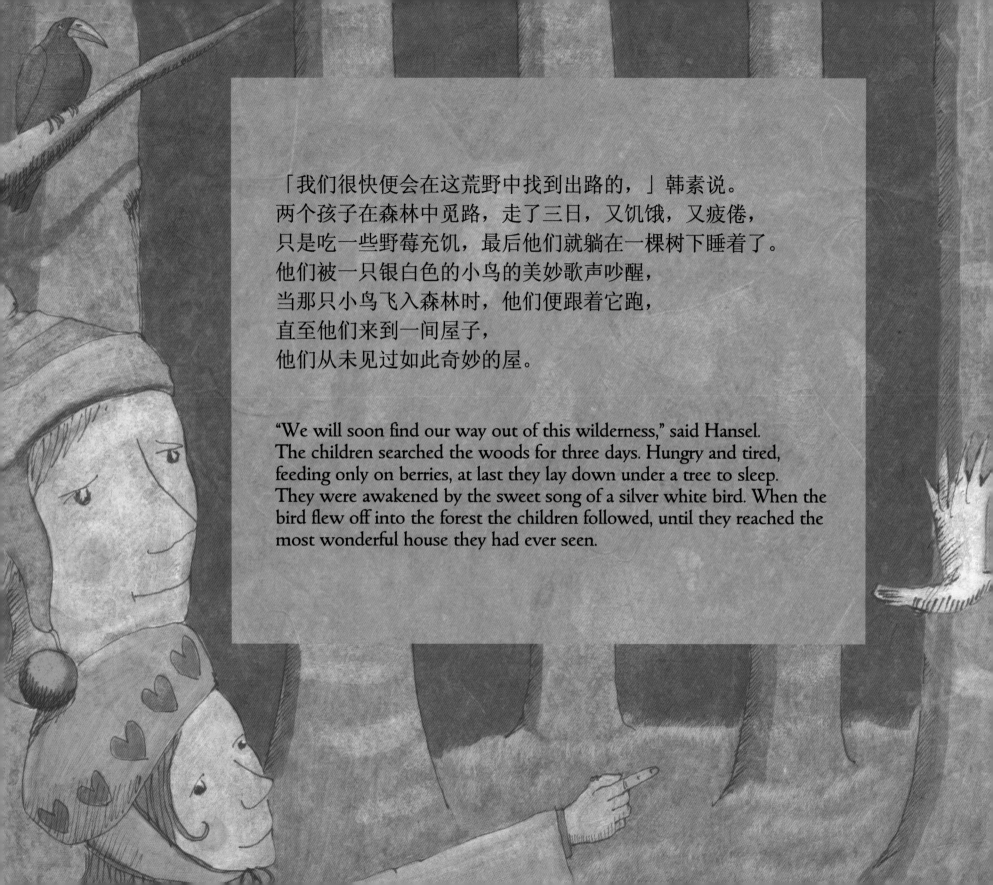

「我们很快便会在这荒野中找到出路的，」韩素说。

两个孩子在森林中觅路，走了三日，又饥饿，又疲倦，

只是吃一些野莓充饥，最后他们就躺在一棵树下睡着了。

他们被一只银白色的小鸟的美妙歌声吵醒，

当那只小鸟飞入森林时，他们便跟着它跑，

直至他们来到一间屋子，

他们从未见过如此奇妙的屋。

"We will soon find our way out of this wilderness," said Hansel.
The children searched the woods for three days. Hungry and tired,
feeding only on berries, at last they lay down under a tree to sleep.
They were awakened by the sweet song of a silver white bird. When the
bird flew off into the forest the children followed, until they reached the
most wonderful house they had ever seen.

The walls were tiled with strawberry tarts,
the roof was made of chocolate hearts.
Around the windows were caramel frames
and the pathway was lined with candy canes.
"Now we can eat!" said Hansel and he bit off
a piece of the roof.
Suddenly, they heard a voice. "Jimney, Jimney,
who's that nibbling at my chimney?"
"It's the wind, it blows right in," they
answered, and went on eating.
All at once the door opened and a strange,
shrivelled woman appeared. Beyond her tiny
spectacles she had blood red eyes.
Hansel and Gretel were so frightened they
dropped their sweets.
"What brought you here, my dears?" she said.
"If it is hunger, then come and see what I
have for you."
She took them by the hand and led them
into her little house.

墙壁是用草莓馅饼堆砌而成，
屋顶是用心型巧克力造的，
窗的周围是焦糖制造的窗框，
而小径则有一排排的糖果棒。
「我们现在可以吃了！」韩素一边说，
一边咬下一块屋顶。
突然他们听到一个声音，「严东，严东，
是谁在咬我的烟囱？」
「是风啊，它吹了进来，」他们答道，
并继续吃。
屋门突然打开，一个又奇怪，
又皱萎的老妇出现，在她那细小的眼镜后面
是一对血红的眼睛，韩素和格妮杜害怕得连
糖果都丢了。
「是什么把你们带到这里来，亲爱的？」
她说，「如果是肚子饿的话，
那么便进来看看我有什么可以给你们吃。」
她拉着他们的手，带他们进入她的小屋。

韩素和格妮杜获得很多很好吃的东西！苹果、果仁、牛奶和铺满蜜糖的薄饼。
跟着他们便倒睡在两张铺了白色床单的床，好像已经到了天堂一样。
那个老妇盯着两个小孩说：「你们两个都太瘦，现在就造美妙的梦吧，
明天你们的恶梦便要开始呢！」
这位有一间可以吃的屋和视力不好的奇怪老妇只是假扮友善，
其实她是一个可恶的女巫。

Hansel and Gretel were given all good things to eat! Apples and nuts, milk, and pancakes covered in honey.
Afterwards they lay down in two little beds covered with white linen and slept as though they were in heaven.
Peering closely at them, the woman said, "You're both so thin. Dream sweet dreams for now, for tomorrow your nightmares will begin!"
The strange woman with an edible house and poor eyesight had only pretended to be friendly.
Really, she was a wicked witch!

到了早上，那可怕的女巫抓住韩素，把他推入笼去，
被困和很害怕的韩素高声求救。
格妮杜立即走过来，「你要把我的哥哥怎么样？」她哭着说。
那女巫一面笑一面滚动着她血红的眼睛，
「我正要将他弄好后便吃了他，」她答道，「你来帮我吧，小朋友。」
格妮杜吓得魂不附体。
她被遣去女巫的厨房工作，要准备特大的食物给她的哥哥吃。
但是她的哥哥拒绝增肥。

In the morning the evil witch seized Hansel and shoved him
into a cage. Trapped and terrified he screamed for help.
Gretel came running. "What are you doing to my
brother?" she cried.
The witch laughed and rolled her blood red eyes.
"I'm getting him ready to eat," she replied. "And you're
going to help me, young child."
Gretel was horrified.
She was sent to work in the witch's kitchen where
she prepared great helpings of food for her brother.
But her brother refused to get fat.

那女巫每天都去看韩素，「伸出你的手指，」她厉声说，
「让我看看你有多胖！」
韩素递出他藏在袋内的幸运叉骨，视力很差的女巫完全不
明白这男孩子为什么会一直都这么瘦。
三个星期之后，她再也按捺不住了，
「格妮杜，快拿木头来，我们要将那男孩子放进锅内，」
女巫说。

The witch visited Hansel every day. "Stick out your finger,"
she snapped. "So I can feel how plump you are!"
Hansel poked out a lucky wishbone he'd kept in his pocket.
The witch, who as you know had very poor eyesight, just
couldn't understand why the boy stayed boney thin.
After three weeks she lost her patience.
"Gretel, fetch the wood and hurry up, we're going to get
that boy in the cooking pot," said the witch.

格妮杜慢慢地推动火炉的火，那女巫忍耐不住，
「火炉应该已经准备好了，走进去，看看是否已经够热！」
她大声叫道。
格妮杜其实知道女巫心中想怎样，「我不知道怎样进去，」她说。
「傻瓜，真蠢的孩子！」女巫怒吼道，「火炉的门已经很阔了，
连我也可以进去啊！」
为了证明她是对的，她便把头伸了进去。
格妮杜快如闪电的将女巫的整个身体推进火炉去，
她把火炉的铁门关上，锁上栓，然后走去叫喊着的韩素，
「女巫已死！女巫已死！可恶的女巫就此没命了！」

Gretel slowly stoked the fire for the wood-burning oven.
The witch became impatient. "That oven should be ready by now. Get inside and see if it's hot enough!"
she screamed.
Gretel knew exactly what the witch had in mind. "I don't know how," she said.
"Idiot, you idiot girl!" the witch ranted. "The door is wide enough, even I can get inside!"
And to prove it she stuck her head right in.
Quick as lightning, Gretel pushed the rest of the witch into the burning oven. She shut and bolted the iron
door and ran to Hansel shouting: "The witch is dead! The witch is dead! That's the end of the wicked witch!"

韩素像小鸟一样从笼里跳出来，

Hansel sprang from the cage like a bird in flight.

韩素和格妮杜互相拥抱，他们唱歌跳舞，欢呼着走来走去。
他们在屋子的每一个角落都找到装满珍珠、绿宝石、红宝石、
以及各种珍贵物品的宝箱，
韩素和格妮杜把他们的袋口都填得满泻。
「我们有奇妙的珍宝，但是我们怎样才能逃离这个野林呢？」
格妮杜叹道。
「不用担心，我们会一起找到返家的路途的，」韩素说。

Hansel and Gretel hugged each other. They danced and sang and ran
around with joy. In every corner they found treasure chests filled with
pearls, emeralds, rubies and all kinds of worldly precious things. Hansel
and Gretel filled their pockets to overflowing.
"We have wondrous treasures, but how do we escape from the wild
wood?" sighed Gretel.
"Don't worry, together we will find our way home," said Hansel.

经过三个小时之后，他们来到一条河。
「我们不能过河，」韩素说，「这里没有船，没有桥，只有清澈的蓝色河水。」
「看！在涟漪上有一只白色的鸭正在游来游去，」格妮杜说，「它或者可以帮我们。」
于是他们一起唱：「有白色闪耀翅膀的白鸭啊，请你细听，
这条河又深又阔，你能否载我们到对岸啊？」
那只鸭子游过来，先把韩素载过去，然后再将格妮杜安全地载过河。
在河的另一边，他们见到的是一个熟识的世界。

After three hours they came upon a stretch of water.
"We cannot cross," said Hansel. "There's no boat, no bridge, just clear blue water."
"Look! Over the ripples, a pure white duck is sailing," said Gretel. "Maybe she can help us."
Together they sang: "Little duck whose white wings glisten, please listen.
The water is deep, the water is wide, could you carry us across to the other side?"
The duck swam towards them and carried first Hansel and then Gretel safely across the water.
On the other side they met a familiar world.

他们一步一步的寻觅回到樵夫的小屋的路。

「我们到家了！」两个孩子高声叫道。

他们的爸爸笑容满面，「你们走后我没有开心过，」他说，

「我到处找你们…」

Step by step, they found their way back to the woodcutter's cottage.

"We're home!" the children shouted.

Their father beamed from ear to ear. "I haven't spent one happy moment since you've been gone," he said.

"I searched, everywhere..."

「妈妈呢？」
「她走了，当再没有任何可以吃的东西时，她怒气冲冲的走了，
说我以后不会再见到她的了，现在就只有我们三个。」
「还有我们珍贵的宝石，」韩素一面说一面伸手入袋取出一颗雪白的珍珠。
「啊！」他们的爸爸说，「我们所有的问题都似乎解决了！」

"And Mother?"
"She's gone! When there was nothing left to eat she stormed out saying I would never see
her again. Now there are just the three of us."
"And our precious gems," said Hansel as he slipped a hand into his pocket and produced a
snow white pearl.
"Well," said their father, "it seems all our problems are at an end!"